He lived in a very busy-looking house which he'd built himself.

As you can see.

It had lots of doors and windows, and do you know what it was called?

Weekend Cottage!

Do you know why?

Because that's how long it took him to build it!

One fine summer morning, Mr Busy was up and about bright and early at 6 o'clock.

He jumped out of bed and had a bath, and cleaned his teeth, and cooked his breakfast, and ate his breakfast, and read the paper, and washed up, and made his bed, and cleaned the house from top to bottom.

By which time it was 7 o'clock.

Busy Mr Busy!

Now, next door to Mr Busy lived someone who wasn't quite such a busy person.

In fact, a very unbusy person.

Mr Slow!

If he was reading this book he'd . . . read . . . it . . . like . . . this!

He'd still be on the first page!

And that same fine summer morning, at five past seven, when Mr Busy knocked at his door, Mr Slow was fast asleep in bed.

He'd gone to bed for an afternoon nap the day before, and somehow hadn't woken up until he heard Mr Busy knocking at his door.

"Who's . . . that . . . knocking . . . at . . . my . . . door?" he called downstairs.

"Good morning," cried Mr Busy. "Can I come in?"

And, without waiting for an answer, he went inside.

"Where are you?" he called.

"Up . . . stairs," came the slow reply.

So Mr Busy went upstairs, two at a time.

"Good heavens!" he said. "You're still in bed!"

And he made Mr Slow get up.

And he made his bed for him, and cooked his breakfast for him, and cleaned his house for him.

Poor Mr Slow.

He hated to be rushed and fussed.

"Right," said Mr Busy briskly. "It's a fine day. Let's go for a picnic."

Mr Slow pulled a face.

"I . . . don't . . . like . . . picnics," he complained.

"Nonsense," replied Mr Busy, and busied himself around Mr Slow's kitchen making up a picnic for the two of them.

It took him a minute and a half.

"Right," he cried when he'd finished. "Off we go!"

And he bustled Mr Slow out of his front door, and off they set.

As you can imagine, Mr Busy walks extremely quickly.

And, as you can imagine, Mr Slow doesn't.

So, by the time Mr Busy had walked a mile, do you know how far Mr Slow had walked?

To his own garden gate!

Mr Busy hurried back.

"Come on," he cried impatiently. "Hurry up!"

"Hurry . . . up?" replied Mr Slow.

"Im . . . poss . . . i . . . ble!"

"Oh, all right," said Mr Busy. "We'll have a picnic in your garden."

"Wait a minute, though," he added. "The grass needs cutting."

And he rushed back to Weekend Cottage and rushed back again with his lawnmower, and rushed up and down cutting Mr Slow's lawn.

It took him two and a half minutes!

It would have taken him two minutes, but he had to mow around Mr Slow who couldn't get out of the way in time.

"Right," cried Mr Busy. "Picnic time!"

And together on that fine summer day they had a fine picnic.

Well, actually, Mr Busy had a finer picnic than Mr Slow because he ate more quickly and had most of the food.

Mr Busy stretched out on the grass.

"That was fun," he said. "I like picnics!"

"You . . . do! . . . I . . . . don't," said Mr Slow.

"Tell you what," went on Mr Busy, ignoring him. "Tomorrow we'll go on a proper picnic, out in the country."

Mr Slow pulled a face.

"And," went on Mr Busy, "in order to do that and get you out into the country, I'll have to call for you earlier than I did this morning."

Mr Slow pulled another face.

"See you tomorrow then," said Mr Busy, and went home and cleaned his house from bottom to top.

The following morning, Mr Busy jumped out of bed at 5 o'clock and had a bath and cleaned his teeth, and cooked his breakfast, and ate his breakfast, and read the paper, and washed up, and made his bed, and cleaned the house from top to bottom.

By which time it was 6 o'clock.

He went and knocked on Mr Slow's front door.

"Come on! Come on!" he cried. "Time to be up and about! Picnic day!"

No reply.

"Come on!" cried Mr Busy again.

No reply.

Mr Busy went inside.

And went upstairs, three at a time, and into Mr Slow's bedroom, expecting to find him in bed.

But he wasn't.

And he wasn't anywhere upstairs.

And he wasn't anywhere downstairs.

"Bother," said Mr Busy. "I wonder where he's got to?"

Where Mr Slow had got to was under his bed.

Hiding!

He didn't want to go on any picnic.

Not he.

"Bother," said Mr Busy again. "That means I'll have to go on a picnic on my own!"

Under his bed, Mr Slow smiled a slow smile.

"What . . . a . . . good . . . idea," he said.

And went to sleep.

Snoring very slowly.

Fantastic offers for Mr. Men fans!

Collect all your Mr. Men or Little Miss books in these superb durable collectors' cases!

Only £5.99 inc. postage and packing, these wipe-clean, hard-wearing cases will give all your Mr. Men or Little Miss books a beautiful new home!

Keep track of your collection with this giant-sized double-sided Mr. Men and Little Miss Collectors' poster.

Collect 6 tokens and we will send you a brilliant giant-sized double-sided collectors' poster! Simply tape a £1 coin to cover postage and packaging in the space provided and fill out the form overleaf.

STICK £1 COIN HERE (for poster only)

cut along the dotted line and return this whole page

Only need a few Mr. Men or Little Miss to complete your set? You can order any of the titles on the back of the books from our Mr. Men order line on 0870 787 1724. Orders should be delivered between 5 and 7 working days.

--- **TO BE COMPLETED BY AN ADULT** ---

To apply for any of these great offers, ask an adult to complete the details below and send this whole page with the appropriate payment and tokens, to: MR. MEN CLASSIC OFFER, PO BOX 715, HORSHAM RH12 5WG

☐ Please send me a giant-sized double-sided collectors' poster.
AND ☐ I enclose 6 tokens and have taped a £1 coin to the other side of this page.

☐ Please send me ☐ Mr. Men Library case(s) and/or ☐ Little Miss library case(s) at £5.99 each inc P&P
☐ I enclose a cheque/postal order payable to Egmont UK Limited for £ ....
OR ☐ Please debit my MasterCard / Visa / Maestro / Delta account (delete as appropriate) for £ ....

Card no. ☐☐☐☐ ☐☐☐☐ ☐☐☐☐ ☐☐☐☐ ☐☐☐☐   Security code ☐☐☐
Issue no. (if available) ☐   Start Date ☐☐/☐☐/☐☐   Expiry Date ☐☐/☐☐/☐☐

Fan's name: ....   Date of birth: ....

Address: ....

....

.... Postcode: ....

Name of parent / guardian: ....

Email for parent / guardian: ....

Signature of parent / guardian: ....

Please allow 28 days for delivery. Offer is only available while stocks last. We reserve the right to change the terms of this offer at any time and we offer a 14 day money back guarantee. This does not affect your statutory rights. Offers apply to UK only.

☐ We may occasionally wish to send you information about other Egmont children's books. If you would rather we didn't, please tick this box.

Ref: MRM 001

cut along the dotted line and return this whole page